Heryin Books
1033 E. Main St., #202, Alhambra, CA 91801
Printed in Taiwan All rights reserved.
www.heryin.com

Text copyright © 2007 by Yang-Huan
Illustrations copyright © 2007 by H.Y. Huang & A.Yang

Library of Congress Cataloging-in-Publication Data
Yang, Huan, 1930-1954. [Chun tian zai na er ya. English]
Where is spring? / Written by Yang Huan
Illustrated by H.Y. Huang & A.Yang,   p. cm.
Summary: "Where is spring? A little boy sends his kite up to ask around...
From field to forest, from far away seas to places nearby"
1. Yang, Huan, 1930-1954--Translations into English.
2. Spring--Juvenile poetry I. H.Y. Huang & A.Yang, II. Title.
PL2922.H8C48 2007 895.1'152--dc22 2006033239
ISBN-10 : 0-9762-0568-8
ISBN-13 : 978-0-9762-0568-5

2/11/88

Where is Spring?

Yang-Huan / H. Y. Huang & A. Yang

heryin Books

Alhambra, California

NORTH END

Spring is here! Where is Spring?

A little boy wonders and wonders, but cannot figure it out:

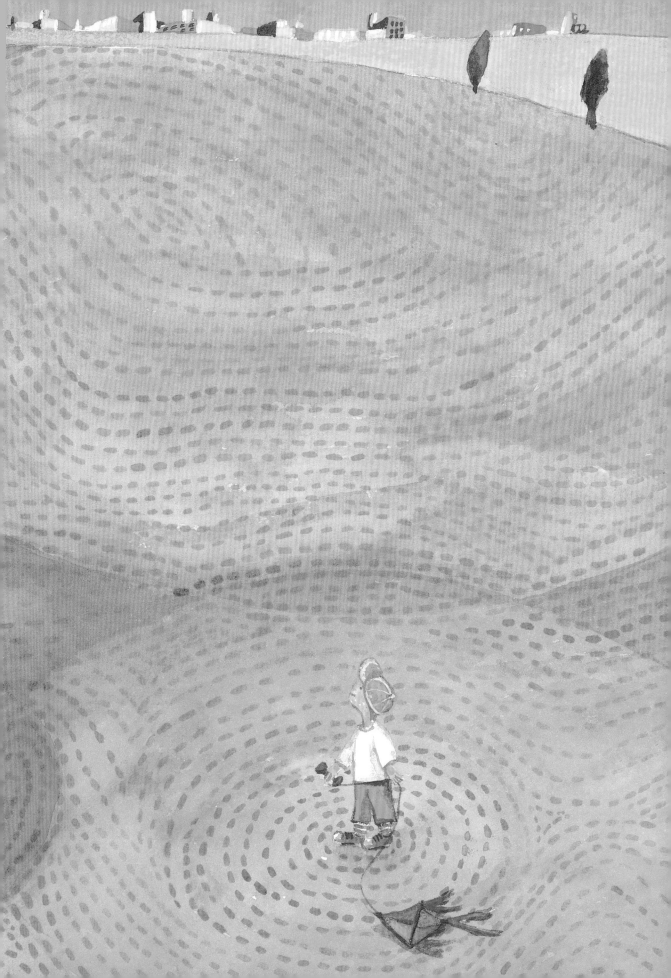

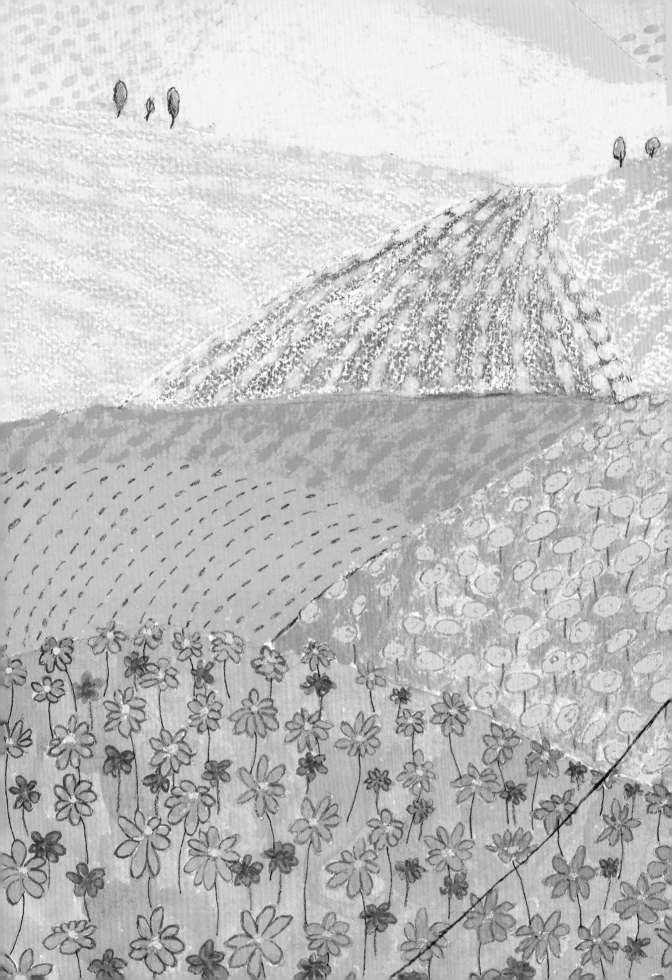

Extending his string
against the southern wind,
He sends his kite
up to ask around.

A seagull says: Spring is traveling by sea in a boat.

Do you not hear the sailors serenading Spring?

A swallow says: Spring is resting in the sky,
Do you not see the busy clouds
Carefully mopping the sky bright and blue?

A sparrow says: Spring is strolling in the fields by the riverbank,

Do you not see the earth awakening from its winter sleep,

Combing the hair of the trees and putting new clothes on the fields?

The Sun says: Spring is burning in my heart,

Spring is smiling on the faces of flowers,

Spring is playing and
studying with kids at school.

Spring is singing and working

along with workers in the factory…

Spring passes through
every bustling street,

Spring walks down every quiet alley.

Lightly Spring climbs over your neighbor's wall,

Lightly Spring enters your home.